Pablo Finds
a Treasure

ANDRÉE POULIN
ISABELLE MALENFANT

annick press
toronto + berkeley + vancouver

Cover art/design by Tatou communication visuelle
Designed by Tatou communication visuelle
Design (English edition): Sheryl Shapiro

Original title: *Pablo trouve un trésor*
Originally published in 2014 by: Les 400 Coups

We acknowledge the support of the Canada Council for the Arts, the Ontario Arts Council, and the participation of the Government of Canada/la participation du gouvernement du Canada for our publishing activities.

Funded by the   Financé par le
Government   gouvernement
of Canada   du Canada

ONTARIO ARTS COUNCIL
CONSEIL DES ARTS DE L'ONTARIO
an Ontario government agency
un organisme du gouvernement de l'Ontario

In Latin America, Asia, and Africa, hundreds of thousands of children work in garbage dumps to salvage recyclable waste. They cannot attend school because they need to contribute to their family's income. More than 150 million children all over the world work in mines, factories, and fields. Half of these children do work that is hazardous to their health. To learn more about child labor, visit http://www.ilo.org/global/topics/child-labour/lang–en/index.htm

Cataloging in Publication

Poulin, Andrée
[Pablo trouve un trésor. English]
     Pablo finds a treasure / Andrée Poulin, Isabelle Malenfant.

Translation of: Pablo trouve un trésor.
Issued in print and electronic formats.
ISBN 978-1-55451-867-8 (hardback).–ISBN 978-1-55451-866-1 (paperback).–
ISBN 978-1-55451-868-5 (epub).–ISBN 978-1-55451-869-2 (pdf)

     I. Malenfant, Isabelle, 1979–, illustrator II. Title. III. Title: Pablo
trouve un trésor. English.

PS8581.O837P3213 2016   jC843'.54   C2016-901883-0
                                                      C2016-901884-9

Published in the U.S.A. by Annick Press (U.S.) Ltd.
Distributed in Canada by University of Toronto Press.
Distributed in the U.S.A. by Publishers Group West.

Printed in China

Visit us at: www.annickpress.com
Visit Andrée Poulin at: www.andreepoulin.ca
Visit Isabelle Malenfant at: lecoindespoolers.com

Also available in e-book format. Please visit www.annickpress.com/ebooks.html for more details.
Or scan

To my fellow author and friend, Mireille Messier.

—A.P.

To my uncle Jacques, for whom all books are treasures.

—I.M.

The sun's first light pierces the sky.
Vultures circle above the shantytown.
Sofia wakes her little brother up.
"Get up! Get up, lazy bones!"
"I'm tired," grumbles Pablo.
"We might find a treasure today," says Sofia.
"I'm tired," repeats Pablo.

Before leaving for the market, Mama reminds them, "Sofia, don't forget the tortillas! Pablo, don't forget your hook!"

The children grab their bags and scurry off to the treasure mountain.

When Pablo and Sofia get to the mountain, lots of people are there already. Pablo holds his nose, even though he knows that in a little while, he won't notice the stink anymore.

Pablo hears the rumble of the motor.
The truck is coming ...
Pablo's heart beats faster.
He feels like reaching for his sister's hand.
He doesn't.
He won't show his fear.

The truck arrives, raising billowing clouds of dust.
Everyone runs.
Some people push.
Some people pinch.
Some people yell.
Pablo hates this rush and crush.

Quick as a flash, Sofia weaves through the crowd.
The first ones to arrive have a better chance of
finding treasures.
Pablo zigzags in the opposite direction.
Someone sticks an elbow in his eye.
The boy falls.
Quickly, he gets up and starts running again.

The truck has emptied its load.
The dust settles.
People stop yelling.
The *pepenadores* dig madly through the latest heap of garbage.
Sofia runs up to her brother.
"Pablo! I found a boot! A blue boot! Your favorite color!"
"Your arm is bleeding," says her brother.
Sofia shrugs. "No big deal. I found my first treasure of the day!"
"This boot is too big for me," says Pablo.
"That's good. You can wear it longer," replies his sister.

Pablo and Sofia gather cans and pieces of glass. With their hooks, they spike bits of plastic and scraps of paper. Later, their mother will sell what they collected for recycling.

Sofia's bag fills up faster than her brother's bag. Pablo is very keen on finding some treasure. He often overlooks recyclable waste.

"Pablo, you missed that plastic container,"
cries Sofia. "Pay attention! If you work hard
today, we might have enough money for
Mama to buy half a chicken for dinner."

Pablo digs up a battered book from beneath a pile of old rags.
"Sofia, I found a treasure!"
His sister makes a face.
"*Pfttt!* That's not a treasure! It won't even buy us three tortillas."
Pablo looks carefully at the illustrations. He wishes he knew what the story was about.
He tells his sister, "I'd like to learn to read."
Sofia shrugs. "What for? Reading won't fill your stomach!"

"*Pstt!* Pablo! Come here! " Sofia takes her brother aside.
"Ta-da! My second treasure of the day!"
She waves two wrinkled carrots. They are a bit soft but
not rotten.
The brother and sister eat the carrots quickly and
silently. On the mountain, it's best to eat any food you
find right away, or someone will steal it.

Suddenly, Sofia yells, "Watch out! Filthy-Face is here!"

All the children flee like wild rabbits.

Pablo and Sofia hide behind a rusted container.
Filthy-Face snatches the bags from the children
who weren't quick enough to hide.
He also makes them empty their pockets.
The little ones cry.
The big ones clench their fists.
No one protests.
No one resists.
Filthy-Face has big fists.
And he hits hard.

Pablo shakes like a leaf in the wind.
He doesn't know if he's trembling with fear or
with rage.

Filthy-Face wanders off.
Pablo takes up his search in the
mountain of trash.
His bag gets heavier.
Sweat stains his shirt.

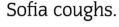

Sofia coughs.
The gases coming off the garbage irritate
her throat.
Tears trace streaks in the dirt on her cheeks.
Pablo wants to comfort his sister.
But he already knows what she'll say:
They're not real tears. My eyes are runny
because of the smoke and the dust.

Pablo is hot and thirsty.
The flies irritate him.
He would love to run and play in the
fountain in the public square.
But the town is too far and his rubbish
harvest is too small.
The boy throws a rock at the vultures circling
above his head and yells,
"Come on, you stinky, dirty old mountain!
Give me a treasure!"

Pablo kicks a garbage bag that has split open.
Oh! There! There, among the potato peels!
He sees something shiny!

Pablo squats and picks through the garbage.
He picks up a chain.
A gold chain!
In his dirty hand, the precious metal shines
like a sliver of sun.
The boy jumps for joy.
He clenches his teeth so he will not scream
his excitement.
He runs to Sofia with his treasure.

Pablo and Sofia hide behind a rusty container.
They whisper their dreams to each other.
They make a beautiful list.
A long list of things they would like to buy once
the gold chain has been sold.

Pablo dreams of
      a book
      a soccer ball
      a new cooking pot for his mama
      an ice cream cone.

Sofia dreams of
      chicken for dinner every night of the week
      a bag of candies
      a new dress for her mama
      gloves to protect her hands when
      she's digging in the garbage.

"Give me the chain. I'll hide it in my shoe," says Sofia.
"No!"
"But your pockets are full of holes," insists Sofia.
"It's MY treasure," says Pablo stubbornly.

"Hey, there! What have you found?"
The children jump up. Sofia screams, "Run, Pablo! Run!"
Filthy-Face chases Pablo.
The boy flees as if fire were burning his heels.
The oversized boot slows him down.
Pablo stumbles and falls in the mud.
Filthy-Face catches up.

Filthy-Face slaps Pablo on the back of the head.
"When I say give, you give. Understand?"
Pablo empties his bag into the thief's bigger bag.
He clenches his teeth so he won't cry.
The man turns his head toward where Sofia ran and yells,
"You, girl! If you don't come back here this second, I'm
taking your brother with me."
Sofia comes running back.
Filthy-Face leaves with all the material collected by
Pablo and Sofia.
He even takes the blue boot.

The children walk home slowly. Sofia yells at her
brother, "I told you to give me the chain!"
Pablo doesn't answer.
"The whole day was wasted," moans Sofia.
Pablo says nothing.
"It's not fair!" whines Sofia.
Tears leave pale streaks in the dirt of her cheeks.
Pablo stays silent.

When the children get home, Mama asks,
"What happened? What's wrong?"
Pablo goes inside and closes the door carefully
behind him.
Finally, he opens his mouth ...